A Sanctuary Christmas

GUARDIANS OF SANCTUARY 5 1/2

TL SHIVELY

There are so many different holidays that are celebrated as well as different traditions with those holidays. They are all special and to them I dedicate this story.

Merry Christmas Bird.

Editing by Partners in Crime Book Services
Book Cover and Interior Formatting by Dreams2media

OTHER BOOKS BY THE AUTHOR

Sanctuary Guardian series reading order:

The Secret Sanctuary

The Town That Time Forgot

The Battle of Sleeping Lady

The Independence Mine Disaster

The Hunter's Betrayal

Haven's Shadow

A Sanctuary Christmas

Spider's trilogy

Spider's Awakening

Also from author:

Sanctuary and Friends coloring book

1

Shadow's Lair

DECEMBER'S cold wind blew Pam's black locks of hair into her face as she stood on the rickety, old-looking porch. She wasn't sure what kept the floor of the porch from crashing down. Flint told her it may look like it could cave in but that it was actually structurally sound. Wearing a leather jacket her brother gave her as well as a dark t-shirt with jeans and heeled boots, she still felt odd being out of uniform. Leaning against one of the posts, looking out over the desolate land around her. The air was cold and frigid but no snow, the trees looked dead and withered even before the cold came.

She had no idea where they were; when she asked her brother, he grinned and said Lucius wasn't the only one who could hide a small population from the world. For someone who hates Lucius as much as Zane seems to, they are so similar in so many ways. When she pointed that out to her brother, he told her to keep that thought to herself. Not like she hadn't figured that out as well. She missed home.

If she was home at Sanctuary, she would be putting up decorations around the Command Center with all the other Arions. Fritz zooming down the halls with his little car all decked out in bells and a wreath. Now, stepping foot on Sanctuary grounds would guarantee her a room in the cell block for rogue Arions, or in the cells in the Omega barracks right next to the Shadows that had been captured.

"Penny for your thoughts…" Her brother joined her on the porch. He had the same dark looks as his sister, his chin dark from stubble. Their outfits almost matched, except the color of his white shirt and the fact that the heels on his boots weren't as high.

"That's probably a bit steep." She looked over at him with a wry grin.

"You're probably right." Flint grinned at her. Even as down in the dumps as she felt, she still smiled. That was the one thing about her brother, he had a way about him that put someone in a cheerful mood. Stazi once told her how that attracted her to him. He put his arm around her and pulled her closer for a brotherly hug. "It's going to be all right, sis. I promise."

"How can you promise that, Flint?" She leaned her head against him, still staring out at the landscape around her. Would make one hell of a Halloween movie. A humorless chuckle escaped at that thought, almost Christmas and she was thinking about Halloween. Wouldn't Cole or Chad get a kick out of that? That thought had her sighing as she moved from her brother's embrace. "I miss our family and my friends." She turned to look at him, her eyes burning. "They believe I've betrayed them; I'm not sure how I feel about that."

"You know…" he started to say but she interrupted him, moving to stand across from him on the porch.

"Yeah, I know, this is the only way to keep Telara and them from dying like the past Guardians." She spoke with exasperation. "But it doesn't help the here and now. Especially since no one will tell me exactly how this is supposed to keep them from dying." Her look became hard as she stared at her brother.

"Naughty Shadows…" The sing-song voice of one of the smaller Shadows interrupted their discussion. Pam turned and watched as the Shadow jumped with each word it sang. "Evil Shadows." The little Shadow stopped and looked up at her with a smile, an eerie smile considering there were no teeth. It reminded her of that animated show Cole and Chad loved to watch with creatures from the Halloween section at the costume store. There were three little gremlins that lived to create havoc in the town, one little girl and her two brothers.

Not only did this little Shadow remind her of the female gremlin with her two pigtails, there were also two other miniature Shadows that resembled the two boy gremlins. One shorter and stockier, while his brother looked lankier with more height. Flint told her the Shadows appeared shortly after her and they were nothing like any of the other Shadows. Pam had to agree, nothing like any Shadow she ever fought, and they had taken a liking to Pam. Something which freaked her out almost as much as the Shadow itself.

The Shadow hopped away, still singing. "Great big blobs of doom." Each hop emphasized each word the Shadow sang.

"It's weird seeing them like this isn't it?" Her brother watched her as she stared at the Shadow. "They don't seem too dangerous here."

Pam frowned at her brother. "Not too dangerous? They tried to kill us."

"Not kill, but capture," her brother corrected her.

"To turn us into Shadows, which we never knew before the Guardians came," she countered.

"But not kill," he persisted.

"We have friends who have been lost, they could be any of these Shadows. Doesn't that bother you?" She knew she was here by her own volition and she shouldn't be getting upset at her brother yet, the fact that he seemed to be defending the Shadows didn't seem to be right to her.

"They will be returned."

"When?"

"When wrong has been righted is what Zane says."

Pam stared at her brother, speechless for a moment before she recovered. "And you can just accept that?"

Flint scoffed. "We were told less in Sanctuary and blindly followed." She opened her mouth to argue but the singing mini-Shadow jumped between them, dancing and singing, not paying attention to either of them.

"I wasn't aware Shadows could talk, let alone sing." Pam gave a shake of her head, blinking as she attempted to process everything happening around her.

Her brother slipped his hands in his pockets, his gaze following her as she started to pace the rickety porch they were standing on. "That one is the first one I know of."

"That one is special."

Pam turned to see Zane leaning against the wooden door frame of the front door. "Why? What makes her special? What makes her different?"

Zane looked behind him into the darkness of the old Victorian house where the Shadow had disappeared and they could still hear her singing her song. "She is one of the first natural Shadows that has been created in such a long time."

"Natural Shadows?" Pam asked.

Zane inclined his head in confirmation.

"What have we been fighting all these years?"

"Manufactured Shadows." Zane tilted his head back, watching as a myriad of emotions crossed Pam's face.

"What is the difference between natural Shadows and manufactured?" She asked him, flinching when one of the hulking Shadows that resembled a large hunchback troll moved past her and leapt off the porch.

"The Shadows your friend Vanna heals are manufactured, they need a living being to exist, which also keeps them stuck within one form." Zane watched the Shadow lumber off into the darkness that surrounded them.

"The shapeshifting Shadows we have been fighting lately are

natural?" Pam wrapped her arms around her stomach staring out into the darkness.

Zane nodded.

"Where did they come from?"

"You were the Alpha leader of Sanctuary." Zane ignored her question as he made his statement. A statement that had Pam narrowing her eyes at him. She said nothing since he spoke a statement, no question asked. "Think you can get into Sanctuary without being detected?"

Pam saw her brother out of the corner of her eye, watching both her and Zane silently. Probably worried that she was about to give Zane some of that attitude she was well known for. She had no plans on rocking the boat, at least not yet but she also wanted to be careful with her words. This wasn't a man to take lightly. "I know of several ways into Sanctuary that no one knows about."

Zane stood straight up and gave a satisfied nod, then turning around he started back into the house.

"Are you really the Shadow Master?" Pam wasn't sure what made her ask the question but before she realized it, the question hung there between them.

Zane turned back around; his eyes lowered making it hard to read his expression as he looked back at her. "Why do you ask?"

"You don't look like you're hundreds of years old." Pam crossed her arms, staring back at him, refusing to back down even as she watched Flint's back straighten.

Zane chuckled. "I'll take that as a compliment." Without answering her question, he headed back into the house, leaving them there on the porch.

"You're the only person I know who would put their well-being on the line just to appease your curiosity." Her brother seemed to relax now that Zane left.

Pam gave a half-hearted shrug. "If you don't ask, then you can't complain when you have no knowledge."

2

Sanctuary

"WATCH OUT!"

CRASH

A pained moan wafted out from beneath the tinsel and ornaments that were strewn across the floor. Gage moved to unbury a groaning Cole as he fought to get untangled from the decorations he had attempted to hang along the walls around the fountain in the Command Center.

As soon as everyone realized he was okay, they laughed while Telara used her mind to move the garland from the floor to drape along the walls with the multi-colored ornaments hanging down every three feet.

"Couldn't you have done that before I ended up on the floor?" Cole slapped the floor with his hand in irritation.

Telara smirked at him. "I could've but it was more fun watching you struggle." Cole glared up at her as Gage pulled him up.

Gage looked around them at all the decorations. Lights were blinking, tinsel and garland were sparkling, as well as the multi-colored bulbs amidst the greenery. They spent the entire weekend decorating the Command Center, all the Faction's quarters and even their bungalow to get into the Christmas spirit. Gage did his best to keep them busy so they were unable to think about the fact that two of their main players were absent from the festivities.

Pam and Lucius.

"Drinks and food in the cafeteria." Gage clapped his hands together to get their attention. They attempted smiles for him although they felt fake. "C'mon guys, everyone else is there waiting for us. We all deserve some cheer." With hesitant nods, they followed him.

They knew Gage was correct but it didn't help the situation. When they first came to Sanctuary several years ago, they had conflicting feelings towards both, while they had their problems with Lucius because of his inability to tell them everything they needed to know, he had become a big part of their lives. Pam had gone from their main antagonist to one of their best friends. She had been one of the main ones trying to figure out to keep them from falling victim to the fate of all Guardians before them.

Hades kidnapped Lucius and the Guardians were forbidden from looking for him by the Leaders. The Leaders were the ones who controlled all at Sanctuary, even Lucius did as they ordered. Not that the Leaders were keeping them from looking for Lucius, it wouldn't be the first time they disobeyed someone in authority, more that they had no idea where to look. They didn't know how to get down to the underworld and even if they could, how would the find him?

Pam had joined the enemy, the Shadow Master whom they met this past summer. Zane, who at the beginning of summer was the commander of Haven, and one who had shown them so much of their own potential. Pam had been the Alpha Leader, now Gage held that position although he still hadn't chosen his second in command. If you listened to rumors, Gage planned to wait until Pam returned, so that she could take her position back. The whole of Sanctuary and all their subsidiaries felt the betrayal. The Alaskan Sanctuary, Rogue Hunters in Illinois,

Haven outpost in Georgia and any that were out there they hadn't been to yet.

"Watch out!" Tobias shouted out to them just in time for them to jump out of the way as Shirk zoomed past them in his tiny car all decked out with bells, garland, bulbs and a wreath on the hood.

The Omega Faction is here? Telara couldn't blame Chance for sounding so surprised, it was a rare occasion that the Omegas come out of their barracks to join with the others. They liked the privacy of not having anyone from the Command Center looking over their shoulders. Looking around the cafeteria they realized that everyone they knew as well as many they didn't, were here. Good thing the cafeteria happened to be one of the largest rooms in Sanctuary.

"I don't think I have ever seen this many Arions in the same room," Tia spoke slowly, looking around them.

Gage cleared his throat before speaking, "This Christmas is a hard one for all of us."

"Don't be a Sally, man!" Trevor winked at them, standing next to Gage with his cap sporting the Hunter symbol.

"Trevor?" Cole grinned at him as they clasped hands in greeting.

"Yeah, Stazi and Lucy are around here somewhere as well." Trevor nodded towards the other side of the room where the two were standing there talking to Travis and Jeff. "Drake, Paul, Wes, Jayne, and some others from Alaska are here as well."

Looking around, they saw Trevor was correct. This wasn't their first Christmas at Sanctuary but definitely the first time they saw so many from all over in one room.

"See ya guys, I need to grab some refreshments before Travis drinks it all." Trevor waved as he trotted to the other side of the room yelling, "Hey, Sally, leave some for me."

Telara couldn't stop the small giggle that escaped as she watched them; the Hunters were an interesting group that never failed to be humorous, whether on purpose or just being themselves.

"We're all trying to get through this together, we've had company from all our sister outposts these past few months at different times," Gage told them, his voice tight with emotion. "Tonight, there will be a bonfire outside the Omega's quarters for everyone to unwind and talk about whatever comes to mind."

"I'll bring the marshmallows." Tia smiled.

"I got the chocolate!" Chad proclaimed.

"Graham crackers!" I.Q. grinned.

"I will bring the heat!" A flame burned in Cole's hand as he stood there with his head held high.

Well, until Chance extinguished it with a shower of water. "I will be there to put out any out-of-control flames." Cole flashed him a baleful look, that he ignored.

"I can provide the marshmallow sticks to be used," Vanna spoke up, to which everyone nodded in agreement. No one wanted to get on her bad side by grabbing a stick that could be considered still living. With everything decided they moved to grab some food, drink and company.

3

Outside the Omega Barracks

"Did you watch *Dead End* last night?"

Tia and Telara both groaned when Chez asked Cole and Chad about their favorite animated show. *Dead End* is a town full of horror type creatures that live together, the mayor of the town was the Grim Reaper named Gerard.

"You mean the tiff between Frank and Stella?" Cole grinned thinking about Frankenstein and his bride from the show.

"That Till started." Chad popped a charred marshmallow in his mouth, one that resembled the Zombie he spoke of in the movie.

"You guys realize that is basically a cartoon?" Tia leaned back in her reclining lawn chair.

Chad, Cole and Chez weren't the only ones that looked insulted at her words. It was Tobias who answered, "Anime, not cartoon." Tobias was the Omega leader, shaven head, dark skin, muscular and not one you would expect that watches cartoons. Tia, Telara, Vanna, Chance and I.Q. stared at him in amazement. He returned their stares with one of his own as he popped a burnt marshmallow in his mouth, then wiped the back of his hand across it.

"How about we change the subject?" Gabe suggested, biting back a chuckle.

"To what?" Vanna looked over at him.

"How about Christmas traditions?" Gabe leaned forward, placing his elbows on his knees as he looked at her intently. "What's yours?"

Snickers were quietly heard all around them as Vanna's cheeks flushed slightly, a pink hue could be seen even in the light from the fire. Most everyone from the cafeteria were sitting around the huge bonfire outside the Omega barracks, others had decided to either adjourn to their quarters or returned to work. Gage told them that he could take them home if they wanted, but they weren't ready to leave yet.

They spent as much time as they could with their family and friends back in Dragoon, after finding out this would be their last year with them, but this holiday season found them needing to be with the family who understood what they were going through. They needed a break from those they loved.

"Usually, we pick an exotic destination we haven't been to yet," Vanna told them, the light pink in her cheeks darkening when conversations around them died down at her words. "My family is sorta … well off," she admitted looking at the charred marshmallow on the end of her stick, sighing. "This year, I managed to convince my family to stay home." She looked back up at everyone. "This is the last Christmas I will be with them and I wanted it to be celebrated at the house I grew up in."

The air went solemn after her words, eyes bright with unshed tears and lips pressed against each other as many found something else to look at. It wasn't the fault of anyone sitting around them that this would be their last Christmas with their families, they weren't even sure who should be the ones carrying that blame.

"We always go to the tree farm just outside of town two weeks before Christmas, we pick out our tree and the family cuts it down. We take it home, warm up with hot chocolate while the tree thaws out in the garage and let it settle overnight. The next day, usually a Saturday, we decorate the tree while singing carols." Tia told them, her gaze on the fire that had started to die with the mood but now became brighter.

"My family gets together the weekend before Christmas to go ice skating, bake cookies and drink eggnog." Everyone turned to look at Tobias, all of them trying to picture him on ice skates but failing. His white teeth flashed in the fire, amusement at their reactions.

"Next you're going to tell us that you dress up your pets for Christmas." Cole scoffed.

"My sister does."

How have you not ended up dead yet? Chance put his head down, shaking it slowly. Cole frowned at him.

How was I supposed to know?

"We go to the tree lighting in the center of town the night of Christmas Eve." Telara stared into the flames, remembering all the times they gathered with the rest of the town all bundled in their winter best, watching the tree light up. The other Guardians nodded, even Vanna had been to a tree lighting ceremony several times in her life.

"My family will still decorate a boat on Christmas Eve." Gage took a bite of his chocolate bar.

"Boat?" I.Q. looked over at him.

"Yeah." Gage inclined his head. "In Greece there is an old tradition of decorating a boat with Christmas lights."

"Why a boat?" Chad now looked interested.

Gage's lips twitched. "Greece is surrounded by the sea."

"Oh." Chad's look went from intrigued to disappointed.

"Not as glamorous a reason as you expected?" Gage raised a brow.

Chad shrugged. "Thought maybe Santa Claus in Greece rode a sea serpent or something like that." The others stared at him. "What?" he questioned defensively. "Could happen. Not like that would be the weirdest thing we ever heard or even saw." When he put it that way, they had to nod in agreement.

4

Gamma Headquarters

CLAW LEANED back in his chair behind his desk, staring at the brightly blue wrapped box sitting on his desk. When they asked him about joining the little party at the bonfire outside the Omega barracks, he had told them he had some work to get done. Truthfully, he just wasn't in the mood to be around others.

"Yeah, that's a lot of work sitting there on that desk. Take you about what? Half an hour to complete. Sure you don't want to take a break halfway through?"

Claw looked up to see Drake standing there with his thumbs hooked into the pockets on his jeans. "Want yer head dunked in a tub of essence?" He growled at him.

Rather than getting upset, Drake's grin broadened. "I would rock a set of fins."

"Ye sound like Cole and Chad," Claw told him grimly, ignoring Drake's reference to Adrijan, the elven prince who became a mentally challenged mermaid after Claw punched him and he fell into a stream full of crystal essence.

Drake tilted his head. "I do it better."

"Did ye have a reason fer being here other than causing me aggravation?"

"Thought you might need a friend." Drake moved further into Claw's office, pulling a chair out for him to straddle, looking at Claw.

"Is that what we are?" Claw's tone belied his belief in those words.

Drake held his hand to his chest giving off an air of faux hurt. "I'm wounded." Claw didn't look a bit amused so Drake dropped his hand with a chuckle. With a sigh, his expression became serious. "Seriously bro, you can't let this tear you down."

"Nothing is tearing me down."

"Really?" Drake leaned back crossing his arms, using his knees to keep him from going too far back as he stared at Claw. "So, it doesn't bother you that Pam joined her brother on the dark side?" A bushy red brow raised at that but when Claw still didn't answer Drake continued, "Wasn't that long ago many worried about you defecting."

Claw's eyes narrowed on him but still he said nothing as he stared at Drake. But Drake refused to back down. "You hardly trusted anyone."

"Because most everyone lied tae us."

"Newsflash, they still are. Pam's as human as we are, she has a breaking point as well."

"Pam follows the rules." Claw looked down at the blue box. "She isnae one tae break them."

"You can't blame her…"

"Aye, I can!" Claw's pained voice drowned out the rest that Drake attempted to say. "She's different. Special. She is the best of us all." His voice softened, something that was so unlike him.

Drake could feel his pain and knew he tread on dangerous ground but he needed answers. "You mad because she left or because she didn't invite you?" The fact that Claw hadn't leapt at him and knocked him on his ass was a testament to how far he had come in the years since him and Pam had separated. "You love her man, you never stopped."

"Ye might wannae rethink yer words." Claw's tone was clipped and terse, letting Drake know that he hadn't come that far and Drake was getting close to ending up on his ass.

"What's in the box?" Drake asked.

"Ye've worn out yer welcome." Claw stood and moved around his desk; arms crossed across his chest.

Drake stood up, turned the chair back around the right way and started for the door that had opened in the wall. Before walking through he paused and spoke to Claw without turning around. "Whether you want to admit it or not, you have friends and we're here for you when you need us." He didn't look to see the reaction from his words, he said what he had to say and now he walked out of the room leaving Claw standing there with the blue box.

5

Shadow's Lair

"HEY, SIS."

Pam had been curled up on a couch in the basement of the Shadow's Lair, flipping through one of the books that had been in Zane's office back in Haven. From everything they learned, the way to save the Guardians was in figuring out the past. These books were full of the past, she just needed to figure out what part this history played in saving the Guardians. Closing the book, she turned her head to watch her brother walking down the stairs.

This ancient looking lair of the Shadows was more than it seemed. The whole structure looked as if one strong wind could tear it down yet it was structurally sound, just as her brother had said. The three small Shadows constantly tumbled around as they wrestled with each other, either that or they would jump and stomp through the lair. Not once did they fall through the floor. The house was so much more than it looked like from the outside, not only structurally sound but the inside was more immense than what it seemed. Along with the three Shadow triplets there were the larger, scarier looking Shadows that lumbered through the house, as well as a Shadow lady who wore a thick white cloak whom she only saw glimpses of; the lady didn't seem to want to be friendly.

This definitely wasn't what she expected.

"Hiding out?" She raised the book she was reading at his question, giving it a shake. "Whatcha reading?" he asked her with a tilt of his head.

"History."

"History?" Flint frowned at her. "You've been out of school for several years now, hell, you didn't like history when you were in school."

Pam swung her legs around, placing her feet on the stone floor and looked at her brother. "The only reason I'm here is to stop the cycle of death and save my friends." Eyes narrowed on her brother as he stood there silently. "Unless your great leader lied to me."

"I leave the lying to Sanctuary." Pam turned to see Zane moving from the shadows of the hallway in the basement that led to the sleeping quarters of all the Arions who were now working for the man standing there.

"Says the man who kept his true identity secret." Pam tossed the book onto the couch next to her and crossed her arms, staring at him with a hard stare. "Did you reveal your identity to the Guardians while you helped *prime* their powers?" The emphasis on the word prime was hard not to miss. By the tightening of Zane's mouth, he didn't miss it.

"Sis." Flint moved off the stairs to stand close to her, the warning in his voice as noticeable as her emphasis on prime.

"She's right," Zane said, though his expression didn't relax. "I had my reasons."

"Really? Sounds exactly like Ira and Lucius."

Zane watched her, his expression no longer as tense. "I'm not holding you here against your will. You're more than free to leave. Though, I doubt your friends would welcome you back with open arms." He moved his arms in an open gesture. "The choice is yours."

"I'm here to protect my friends, you told me that this was the only way to save them."

Zane nodded.

"Then here I stay. But know this, if you lied to me and my friends end up hurt, your Shadows won't be able to protect you from me." Pam didn't rise from her seat, her voice stayed steady but her expression showed the myriad of emotions that she felt.

Flint watched between the two, his stance guarded as his head moved back and forth as they spoke. He didn't relax until Zane grinned as he started speaking, "Now that that's settled, I have a mission for you two."

"And if I don't agree?" Pam spoke up and Flint stared at her, his eyes widened as if to ask if she lost her mind. Maybe she had.

"You know where the door is." Zane stared at her as she stared back, neither flinching or looking away.

"What do you need?" Flint queried, pulling both their attention from their staring contest.

"Christmas Eve is less than a week away." Pam said nothing, after all, Zane spoke a fact, not a question. "Sanctuary still go caroling through Thetis on Christmas Eve?"

Pam's head inclined slowly, it should've surprised her that Zane had this information but considering how many Arions she had seen around her that had disappeared years ago, she was sure he had more information than just that. "Calanda. An old tradition carried on by our ancestors during their time in this land, something to bring a bit of home with them." Most of Sanctuary are either Greek or of Greek descent.

"I know." She frowned at Zane, who looked amused. "I wasn't always the Shadow Master."

That comment garnered Pam's attention. "So, you're not the original Shadow Master. Was the title given to you or did you take it from another?"

"You could say that," Zane answered her but then continued as if the subject was closed. "When the Calanda happens, the Command Center is left with a skeleton crew, correct?"

"The Command Center is always protected," Pam informed him tartly but then amended, "But there won't be as many."

"What about where the Shadows who haven't been healed are kept?"

Pam frowned at him. "Why?"

"Answer the question."

Pam's lips thinned and her eyes went hard as she stared at him, her words were spoken curtly, "The Omega's barracks should be completely deserted, they would have an alarm system armed but no personnel."

"I need you to get me one of the unhealed Shadows."

Pam's eyes widened before her expression cleared, although her posture stayed tense as she spoke, "how do you know which ones of the Shadows were unable to be healed?"

"I have my ways." He stood there watching her. "You will get me the one I want and bring him back here."

Pam scoffed, "The Shadows aren't the friendliest of creatures."

Zane tossed a blackened crystal tower to her that she caught in her hand. There in the center of the tower was a small black tornado that seemed to swirl from the base to the center of the tower. Clear liquid swirled with the darkness and white wisps. She looked back up at him, her mouth slightly open but no words came as she looked back down at the crystal tower in wonder as he spoke. "That will keep the Shadow docile and easily controlled."

Her expression didn't clear up at his explanation. "And how will I know which Shadow you want? Or am I supposed to bring back all the Shadows?"

Zane didn't miss the sarcasm so heavily laced in her words, the narrowing of his eyes told her that, even if he didn't address it.

"The crystal will lead you to the one I want, then the crystal will make sure you're able to get him to do as you command him."

"Him?" Pam frowned at him; she never heard anyone give Shadows any type of humanity until after they were healed.

"Slip of the tongue," Zane said dismissively. "If you're unable to do this, I can find another, although it will make me wonder what use you will be to me."

Pam's arms crossed. "What's to stop me from using this to command other Shadows against you?"

She heard the sharp intake of breath from her brother. "Sis!"

Zane held up a calming hand, his eyes not leaving Pam's face. "Best to get this out in the open now. That crystal is linked to that one Shadow, it will only work with him."

"Don't trust me?" Pam tilted her head.

Zane snorted at that question, shaking his head with a sardonic expression. "About as much as you trust me."

"Fair enough." Pam couldn't argue with that logic.

"Get my Shadow and bring him to me, then we can discuss the possibility of future trust." With those words he turned and walked out.

Zane looked at his sister with a slack-jawed expression. "What's up with you? You never used to be this combative."

"Telara must be rubbing off on me." Pam shrugged, staring down at the crystal tower.

"Regretting your decision?"

Pam looked up from the crystal to her brother who stared at her. "Could be that too."

"Be careful, sis." Flint spoke gently to her. "This isn't the Sanctuary and Zane isn't one to be played for a fool."

Telara's Home

"Thank you for helping with cleanup, hon."

Telara helped her mother clean after dinner, something she used to balk at. It only took them a total of twenty minutes to clear the table, put away the leftovers, rinse the dishes and put them in the dishwasher. Had she truly complained about taking twenty minutes out of her day to help her mother? Yes, she had. It really hit home when her mother thanked her for helping.

Her lips curled into a self-deprecating smile. "You don't have to thank me, Mom. I enjoyed it." Her mother raised an eyebrow at that last comment, Telara couldn't hold back the half-chuckle. "Was nice helping and talking." She finished lamely but she was being truthful, while they cleaned they not only talked about when her and Ra were young but her mom also told her stories about her youth as well as early dating stories with her father.

"I did too." The smile on her mom's face lit her features right up. Telara had to look away so that her mom wouldn't see the brightness in her eyes. "Everything is done for the night, there is still time for you to go hang out with your friends before bedtime."

Her head tilted as if she thought about it before she gave a slow shake of her head. "Nope! I'm good. Would rather spend time with you, Dad and Ra. Maybe we can make some sugar cookies like we used to." The quick turn of her mom's head in her direction and widening of eyes showed surprise at Telara's comment.

A snort from behind her had her turning to see her sister standing there with winter coat, glove, hat and scarf in hand. "You stay with Mom and Dad but I have plans with Cheryl at the Wolf's Den."

"C'mon, Ra, how long's it been since we baked and decorated sugar cookies?" Telara implored her sister.

Tiara paused in the middle of sliding on the heavy winter jacket giving Telara a slanted look. "You're serious?" Telara nodded. "We stopped helping with baking of sugar cookies back in middle school, you know, when you said that was for kids who had nothing better to do."

"Well, I was wrong," Telara said, holding up her chin for emphasis.

"Until Tia or one of the others call." Her dad walked into the kitchen with a smirk as he grabbed a can of pop from the fridge.

"Actually, I believe they are spending time with their families too," Telara countered.

Her dad looked over at her mom. "Must be something in the water." Her mom laughed but smiled in agreement with her dad.

"Must be."

"Can't I want some family time without you guys thinking I'm on drugs?" Telara protested, placing her hands on her hips as she frowned at her parents with an offended air.

Her dad held up his hands in mock surrender. "You can't blame us for being caught unaware, kiddo. You kids don't have the best track record for wanting family time."

Telara bit her bottom lip, knowing her dad spoke the truth. Usually, she only gave her parents as much time as she had to before rushing off to spend the rest of her time with friends. Now that her time with her family was coming to an end, she hated being away from them. It took knowing they only had borrowed time for her to realize how precious that time was. "Won't kill us to give up one night." Telara gave Tiara a pleading look.

Tiara groaned and gave a deep sigh. "Fine! But I'm blaming you when Cheryl asks why I didn't come."

Telara wasn't the only one laughing at that. "I'm good with that, everyone blames me for your faults anyways."

Tiara grinned unabashedly. "Yeah, they do. Not that I'm complaining or anything."

The room filled with laughter as they pitched in to get the ingredients out for sugar cookies. They laughed, made messes and even let their mom take pictures. The house, warmed from the oven's heat, smelled of delicious sugar cookies, the atmosphere full of joy and laughter.

Shadow's Lair

"CONTROLLED SHADOWS…" Kele, the female Shadow of the mini trio, stomped through the hallways as she sang that song of hers. Her voice, while being soft, carried through the whole house. Shadows of all sizes and shapes lumbered past her, most moving out of her way although some of them would knock her out of their way. Pam wasn't sure why she felt angry at that, but she had a hard time not pulling out her Crim and showing the bullies some respect. "Scary Shadows … Gloom … Gloom … Gloom!" Although Kele didn't seem fazed as she continued singing and jumping with each gloom she sang.

"You seem in deep thought."

Pam turned to see the robed woman standing there watching her, she had wondered if she would come face to face with the woman or not. She had heard everything about her during the Guardians' time in Alaska, and heard that they thought whatever this woman attempted to do had also healed Gage. Whether it had been the woman's intention or not, no one knew. "You could say that," Pam answered her but said nothing more.

"Trying to figure out how you can easily live among creatures that you have been taught to hate your whole life?" The woman watched her with a serene smile on her face. The smile looked innocent enough but it also gave Pam shivers that she hoped didn't show. The woman looked so frail, a good gust of wind could blow her into the next county, except Pam knew she was capable of much more. The saying, never judge a book by its cover, came to mind.

"You could say that."

"I did say that." The woman moved closer; the only noise was the bottom of her cloak brushing along the decrepit looking floor. With most everyone else, the floor creaked with their weight, but not with her. "What brings you here if you are so uncomfortable around the Shadows?"

Before Pam could answer, Zane appeared. "That is between her and I."

The woman stopped and turned to look at Zane. "Is that so?"

"Yes." Zane's response was curt, his expression as stiff as his posture. Pam didn't say anything but watched silently as the woman stopped just a few feet from him. No words were said as they stared at one another, Pam wondered if there was going to be an altercation right there in the hallway.

Looking around she noticed that the Shadows that had been ambling around the house had gone eerily still, their focus on the two staring at each other. Would they attack the woman if she and Zane got into an argument? Would Zane stop them if they did? Thankfully, those questions didn't need answered as the woman turned away from him and walked past Pam, disappearing through a doorway. Pam looked back towards Zane but he had disappeared as well.

"And Sanctuary has all the secrets?" Her sarcasm was wasted on the empty air around her.

8

Sanctuary

"THAT LOOKS LIKE A TWO-YEAR-OLD WRAPPED IT!" Vanna stood there with her hands on her hips staring at Cole's attempt at wrapping presents.

Cole frowned up at her. "They're going to tear the paper off anyways, it doesn't need to look perfect," he protested as Vanna grabbed the package from him, ripping off the paper while throwing baleful looks at him before she started wrapping the box herself.

"When will Vanna realize he does that on purpose? So she'll wrap it for him?" Tia leaned back in her chair next to Telara as they watched the scene unfold. Cole leaned back in his chair watching Vanna, barely holding back his pleased grin.

"I think she knows," I.Q. told them as he finished his sixth present tossing it in the pile with the others. Sanctuary bought gifts and wrapped them for everyone in Thetis, Tobias would dress up as Santa Claus, delivering the gifts on a sleigh with Gamma upgrades.

"The funny thing is that no one in Thetis even believes in Santa but they won't confess to that because they like getting the free gifts." Gage sat on the table next to them grinning as he watched them wrapping the gifts.

Chance hopped up onto the table next to Gage, grimacing when two rolls of wrapping paper rolled onto the floor making colorful trails. "I think Chad and I almost gave our parents a heart attack when we told them we wanted to spend some time with them."

Gage frowned at him but the other Guardians knew exactly what he was talking about. "My dad kept trying to take my temperature when I suggested we spend some time together." I.Q. admitted. "But he still got out the Uno cards while I made the hot chocolate." His lips quirked with the memory

"My mom actually gave up her spa night she had planned." Vanna put the last piece of tape on the box she wrapped and then placed it gently on the pile. "We went sledding out at Tempest Hills. Thadius got to try out his new sled."

"What?" Chad jerked, looking at her through wide eyes. "Your mother risked messing up her hair to go sledding?"

Vanna nodded with bright eyes. "She said if I could take time away from my friends, then she could risk some frizz."

Everyone went silent. Vanna's mother wasn't one to do anything that risked messy hair, dirt getting on her clothes or even worse, a broken nail. They never doubted their parents loved them, not once. What they didn't realize was how much their parents valued spending time with them. Until now, when their time was becoming limited.

9

Shadow's Lair

PAM STARED down at the miniature crystal tower in the palm of her hand, watching the blackness inside the crystal still swirling. She thought about how Claw would love to get his hands on this. Even before it was proven, he believed that there was more to the crystals than what they had been taught. After the Guardians came and freed the Rotary, Claw was able to prove the essence could be controlled and exonerated his ancestor.

"Worried they might cancel Calanda this year?"

Pam turned to look up at her brother, her lips quirking. "Nope."

"Why is that?"

"I know how the Command at Sanctuary thinks." Pam tilted her head. "When things feel as if they are spiraling out of control, you control what you can and let the rest fall into place."

Flint nodded. "I get that." He frowned when Pam giggled. "What was that about?"

Pam shook her head, still laughing. "Just remembering the first time the Guardians participated in Calanda."

"Oh?" Flint looked interested. "Do tell."

"Vanna had to bring Streak with her, a squirrel made completely from a silver liquid metal who had a connection with her. She would bring him with her wherever she went in Sanctuary." She bounced the crystal in her hand. "He was fine for the most part, until we gathered outside the Cantina. He went spastic, couldn't keep his form, and finally Vanna took him back to their bungalow, putting him back into the power room where he finally settled down."

"Power room?"

Pam lifted a shoulder. "They have a room downstairs in their bungalow, a room so vast that it is as if there is another Sanctuary within. They practice their powers there and that is where they discovered Streak."

"Has she tried taking Streak caroling after that?"

Pam gave a shake of her head. "After that, Vanna didn't take him out in Sanctuary again. Left him in the Power room."

"Hmmm." Flint watched as her thumb moved slowly across the surface of the small tower. "You know, you can leave the crystal in your room until we leave. You don't need to carry it with you everywhere you go."

"I know. It seems so unnatural for a crystal to have black in it." She gave a disparaging grin. "Not that anything about our lives is natural."

"The only crystals you see are the ones that have been vetted and buffed by the Gamma Faction. There could be others like that one." Her brother inclined his head towards the crystal tower. "You just might not know about it."

Pam half chuckled, half snorted. "If Claw saw anything like that, the whole of Sanctuary would know."

"Maybe." Flint lifted a single shoulder with a slight twist of his lips.

"What do you mean, maybe? He's always trying to prove there is more to the crystals than we were taught."

He nodded. "Yeah, and each time he was treated with disdain

or as if he was being a conspiracy theorist." He watched her closely. "Even by his girlfriend."

Pam glared at him. "That's not fair, we didn't know back then."

"Everyone does now, I wonder if he ever got an apology." When the only answer was silence he sighed. "Didn't think so."

Pam took a deep breath before changing the subject. "So, you're saying all our crystals could have blackness in them and we wouldn't know?"

Flint slanted his head slightly. "I don't know. According to a woman who lives here with the Shadows, the crystals at Sanctuary were manufactured, so they won't hold the true power of the crystals."

"The woman in the cloak?" Pam queried watching her brother.

"You've met her?" Flint frowned.

Pam lifted a careless shoulder. "Briefly but Zane seemed to chase her away."

Flint nodded. "They have a kind of odd relationship."

"Does she have a name?"

This time it was Flint who lifted an uncertain shoulder. "If she does, she hasn't shared it."

Pam looked down at her Crim still attached to her belt, then looked back up into the darkness of the hallway where they were standing. Her brother put his arm around her and gave a gentle squeeze. "Things will work out, sis. You'll see."

"Yeah."

10

Sanctuary

"Aᴍ I the only one feeling like a complete jerk?"

Telara's head jerked up at I.Q.'s question, her brow furrowed as she attempted to figure out what he was talking about.

"Our parents dropped everything when we asked about getting together." His self-deprecating smile felt within all of them. "Are we really that terrible?"

"Our mom acted like she won the lotto." Chad leaned forward, placing his chin on the knuckles of his clasped hands. His brother nodded with a faraway expression on his face.

"Isn't that what teens do though?" Cole reasoned.

"But does it make it right?" Tia looked around at them all.

"You're teens who have a clock counting down on your backs." Gage entered their common room in their bungalow. Since Pam's defection, he had become their confidant in the Command Center. "After all you've been through, cut yourself some slack."

The room went silent, each of them lost in their own thoughts. Thoughts that they shared, all along the same lines. Never once thinking twice when they chose to hang out with each other and school friends over their family. Now, with their time limited, they only wanted more time with their families.

"Have you talked with Zach since Georgia?" Cole looked over at Telara.

"Nope." One simple word spoken, though one full of much emotion. "For once, my dreams have been completely peaceful." She snorted. "Even Kyler has left me alone."

"Has anyone seen the two new Paladins?" Gage asked. When they shook their heads in answer, he attempted to ease the tension. "Maybe they're all giving you space." When they didn't react to his words, he sighed. "Any normal person would've folded going through what you have through the past two years or so."

"You calling us normal?" Chad looked bemused.

Telara looked over at Chad, her lips curled. "What normal person that you know can make their own ice cubes?"

Chad inclined his head slightly. "Fair enough."

Cole frowned at Gage. "How are you so unaffected by this? Your leader and good friend just switched sides."

"Cole." Tia admonished him with a gust of air that only blew his hair back instead of knocking him out of his seat, like she normally did. That, in itself, was telling of their moods.

Gage lifted a hand to her. "That's all right, he has a right to ask." Gage shrugged. "I grew up in Sanctuary, we have watched friends go down more times than we cared. We believed back then that many were completely lost to us, although some we knew had defected to the darkness. Unlike you lot, we weren't just thrown into this world. But that doesn't mean we weren't affected, just that we have learned how to handle ourselves when needed."

"So, you were upset?" Vanna peered at him.

He nodded at her.

"Doesn't show." She didn't look away as she spoke.

"You haven't seen the wall in my room." Silence followed that remark. "I'll have many questions for Pam when we come face to face again."

"Not if?" Tia turned to look at him.

"Nope, we will." There was confidence in his words. "Until then, we'll move forward. Wallowing in despair won't help. It will only lead to more darkness." He moved away from them and towards the doorway. "Let's head over to Thetis, the Calanda will be starting soon."

Vanna looked at Cole with her piercing eyes. "Wonder why Kull never asked about your brother; he is your father after all."

Cole's jovial mood evaporated as his face darkened while he grumbled into his hot chocolate. "I was avoiding that part."

Tia gave a slight shake of her head. "Should forgive rather than hold your anger in, it's not healthy. Besides, he did help draw out your power," she reasoned but Cole's face was still dark as he glowered at her.

"Should we talk to your parents to see if they feel the same?" he asked her.

Her shoulders lifted. "I don't believe we have met either of mine." She looked at Telara. "Have we?"

Before Telara could answer her, Gage interrupted. "I'm confused, these are your ancestors, right? You're talking as if they are you."

"Honestly, we're not sure what to think." Telara admitted. "But we believe that we're the reincarnations of the children of the Paladins."

"And the Paladins were the first Guardians?" Gabe asked.

"Not really." Telara sighed. "It seems as though the Paladins were from another planet, realm or something like that. And they didn't bring the Shadows with them. There are still so many unanswered questions." Her voice was heavy with emotion and weariness from all that they had been through.

"So, if you are reincarnations of your past selves, does that mean you'll get the memories of your past selves and be different?" Gage's eyes darted between all of them. "Will you become them and not you anymore?"

Telara looked at Tia then at the others with wide eyes, she had never thought about that. "Not sure."

"Hope not." Vanna frowned at the thought.

"Me too." Gabe's face looked troubled. "I like you guys as you are."

"Any way to find out what will happen?" Gabe asked, moving

closer to Vanna with a worried look. They gave slow shakes of their heads; they truly didn't know.

"What about your dream guy?" Trent asked her.

That got a derisive snort from her. "He's hiding."

"Hiding?" Gage looked at her.

"That's all I can say for sure since he hasn't visited my dreams since before we went to Georgia." Telara stopped and looked up into the sky. "Thankfully, neither has Kyler. Not sure how much longer that will be though. Although, one could hope." The other Arions decided to not press her anymore, to which she was thankful, as they moved deeper into Thetis where they met with the others before heading to do their caroling.

12

Shadow's Lair

PAM MOVED from the basement where she had been spending most of her time reading all the books Zane had allowed her. Which was any book in his library so far, but never more than two at a time. Heading upstairs and moving through the hallways, unsure of her destination, just wanting out of the basement. Back at Sanctuary she barely had time to just sit and read, before the Guardians came to Sanctuary, she spent most of her time with her Alpha Faction either training to keep their senses sharp or making sure the world was safe from the Shadows. She sighed, she missed her friends, all of them. She truly didn't realize how hard this was going to be.

She turned a corner to see the hallway split in two, one curved off to the left while the other went straight down. She stood there momentarily looking between the two, a movement down the hallway that curved made her decision for her. She moved down the straight hallway looking into the rooms that had open doors but saw sitting rooms with furniture and a kitchen that looked eerily clean with up-to-date appliances. When Flint first brought her here, she was sure this was the place they chased him to, back in Illinois, but the inside of that house was normal, nothing like this. One room was as large as their training gym back at the Command Center with work out equipment that just like the appliances in the kitchen, looked very out of place in this Halloween like house. When she told Flint how odd it was to see normal looking rooms in this place, whatever normal was in their world, Zane had overheard and laughed at her. "What did you expect to find?" He had asked her. "A mad scientist lab with torture rooms and a dungeon?" She wasn't sure how to answer that, considering that was exactly what she had expected to see, so she had stayed quiet.

Looking back down the hallway that she was walking down she had a sinking feeling she probably should've left a trail of string or something to find her way back to the basement. Her brother would be coming to get her soon for their mission, the thought had her stomach clenching. Closing her eyes, she took a deep breath, muttering to herself, "You can do this, you *have* to do this."

She was going deeper into the Shadow's Lair, as she had come to call this place, than ever before. Turning back around, she bit back a scream as she almost ran into a Shadow that stood there, one she knew wasn't there moments before. She had to suppress a shudder when one of the snake-like Shadows slithered by her on the floor, her hand positioned close to her hidden Crim. While most of the Shadows she saw were the shapeshifting ones that gave her chills, she had seen some of the ones she fought before for so long, the minions and even a few generals that could possibly be fallen comrades. Another point of contention that she had been wrestling with.

Ducking into a nearby doorway, Pam avoided a huge spider Shadow that crawled along the wall of the hallway. Taking a deep breath she turned further into the room, going still as she felt as if she had just walked into one of those old-time horror flicks. Here was the mad scientist lab Zane joked about, although she wasn't laughing.

"Hello there."

Standing on the other side of the room, a very pale hand resting on the metal table she was next to, was the same cloaked woman she had met in the hallway. The one that Flint said had no name. On the surface of the table next to her were several sinister looking implements, whose purpose she wasn't sure she wanted to know. Especially considering the gurney in the middle of the room with leather cuffs at the foot and on the sides.

"What is this place?" She looked back at the woman.

"I think you know."

Pam crossed her arms leaning back slightly watching the woman, who watched her from beneath her cloaked hood. "Humor me."

A slight tilt of the woman's head had Pam smirking. "That's Zane's job, not mine." Pam was sure the woman didn't like her being there, she just wished she knew why.

Pam looked around the room as things started to click inside her mind. "This is where Telara saw you turn Gage into a Shadow."

Pam could see just a fraction of the woman's face, her skin so translucent that she wondered if it wasn't the woman's bones she saw. "Not I, that was Jasper." A soft sigh could be heard. "The poor dear, our newest members of the family have made him somewhat … obsolete."

"Your words don't match your tone." Pam straightened, watching the woman.

"They don't? I'll have to work on that." Pam had a feeling the woman was being sarcastic but her tone barely changed its pitch or reaction.

"So, you're no longer turning people into Shadows?" Pam figured if the woman was going to talk to her might as well get as much information as she could.

The cloak moved so slightly when she raised a shoulder in response to Pam's question. "Why should we? When the natural

Shadows are being created in more abundance, although I have to say the manufactured Shadows tended to listen better."

Pam's hand moved to her stomach hearing the woman speak so callously about the Shadows created from friends and innocents. "Those are my friends you're talking about."

This time the woman turned to look straight into Pam's face, letting Pam see her full face that was the same translucent color. Her eyes were a washed out purple, hair so white it looked as if she had no eyebrows or lashes. The woman was what nightmares were made of. "You mean they were your friends, don't you?"

Before Pam could answer, Flint opened the door that Pam hadn't realized had closed. "There you are sis, we need to get going."

Pam nodded at him, turning back to where the woman had been just seconds before, but now she was gone as well as the implements that Pam had seen on the table. "Where did she go?"

"Who?" Flint frowned at her.

"Forget it, let's get this over with." She moved past him into the hallway, not really looking forward to what they were about to do.

13

Thetis

"You knew the original Paladins and their children." Telara leaned against the bar where Serdita was drinking with Silest. Their metal mugs were steaming although the steam was twirls of rainbows rising from the cups. Silest slithered away as Serdita turned to look at her.

"I did?" Nothing in her expression gave her reaction away as she looked at Telara, her lips curling into a smile. Her wings settled against her back.

"Yes, and you counseled them."

A raise of an elegant brow rose at Telara's words, the only reaction she got but it was enough. "Is there a point to this?"

"Why won't you help us?"

"Who says I haven't?"

It seemed as if every other day Telara had to face frustration from one source or another; aggravation had become an old friend that had worn out its welcome. Every time they managed to get a few steps ahead, something would happen to knock them several steps back. No matter how optimistic she tried to be, reality always came crashing around her. With all the opposition they've been dealing with on a regular basis, no one could blame her for the foot stomp she couldn't contain. "Can't anyone give us straight answers?" She practically growled, Serdita watching her, a grin starting to appear on her face.

"It's good to see your mother's bite hasn't faded after all this time," was Serdita's amused response, the smile on her face broadening at the confusion on Telara's.

"Huh?"

"Enjoy this year, an unspoken truce has come to pass that will give you something no other Guardian before you have had, peace." Telara just stared at her, not sure what to say. "When the year is over, come see me. Then we will talk." Serdita raised a hand when Telara opened her mouth to speak. "This isn't up for debate. When you leave your home, when you close that door, your new life will begin. Only at the end can you begin."

The last sentence was spoken so low that Telara wasn't sure she had heard her right. Even so, nothing Serdita said made much sense to her. What unspoken truce? She knew the Leaders had said that they had this last year with their family and friends from the outside, but they said nothing about a truce. Does Serdita know more than the Leaders? Telara looked over at her friends who were laughing with Gage, Gabe and some of the satyrs over at a table, then back to Serdita. "How do we go back home and act as if everything is normal? Knowing at the end of the year it will be over?"

For a moment Telara thought that Serdita had felt some compassion for what they were going through, then she spoke, "if it's too much then we can arrange for it to end now. You won't have to go back to your family and we can start your education in earnest." Her tone was spoken as if she was speaking of what was on the menu.

It took Telara a few moments to speak, her throat tightened with emotion. "Do you have any feelings about this?" Telara stared, wide-eyed at Serdita, her head slowly moving back and forth in disbelief.

"Of course I do, but I can't let them interfere with the mission."

Telara felt as if she was talking with Kyler. "I don't care about your mission; I care about my family."

"My mission is to save this world, one your family lives in, so I would think you would care as well. So, I ask again. Do you want to start your final education and training now or after you graduate?"

Her lips pressed together, Telara responded through her tight lips, "Graduate."

Serdita gave a nod that gave none of her thoughts away, turned around, moved forward into the crowd of Arions, Satyrs and other residents of Thetis. Tia moved closer to Telara and wiped a tear that Telara hadn't noticed from her cheek. "This isn't fair." Telara's voice cracked.

Tia hugged her friend closely. "No, it's not," she agreed.

Cheering had them turning, Telara hastily wiping the wetness from her cheeks, to see the Grendow sisters walking in grinning with several gnomes and satyrs carrying in barrels with the words Grendow Ale etched into the wood.

"Aly!"

"Jamma!"

The whole cantina erupted into cheers for the sisters who were grinning big as their barrels were carried behind the bar into the back room. Aly with her braids flying around her and her sister Jamma with her signature bandana holding back her fly away hair that was as untamable as she.

"New pair of boots you got there, Aly?" Cole moved closer to Aly, who climbed up onto a stool by the bar where Daphne was setting her up a tankard that was half the normal size, specially made for their patrons whose size was on the smaller side. Aly looked up at him as she took a long swig.

"Thanks." She turned away from him to talk to her sister who gave Cole side eyed looks.

"I mean it," he told her earnestly, leaning against the bar next to her, smiling down at her. "Ouch!" He went from charming to hopping around on one foot after Tad stomped on the other one.

The sisters giggled as they hopped down off their stools. "Time for Calanda!" Jamma hollered, heading out the door into the suddenly brisk air. Christmas magic is what they called it, for one night and one whole day every year, Sanctuary gets to experience the cold of a Christmas Eve and day. It will even snow, leading to snow gnomes and snow ball fights.

"What was that about?" Vanna asked Cole as she helped him to one of the stools more built for a "normal" sized occupant.

Cole gave a half-hearted shrug and a smirk. "Was kind of hoping to get her to let me have some of that ale of theirs, I keep hearing the gnomes and satyrs saying how good it is."

Vanna's eyes narrowed as she shoved him off the stool.

"Hey!" He frowned up at her.

"Do you even listen to yourself half the time?" Vanna looked crossly at him, her hands on her hips. "Either of you?" Chad started to protest when her cross look turned to him.

"How did I get pulled into this?"

"You two always work as a team, I'm sure you had your sticky fingers in that stupid scheme as well." Vanna pinned him with a look, effectively silencing any more protests. "You guys are so uncouth."

"Uncouth?" Chad looked at Cole, then I.Q., who kept his distance. "What does that mean?"

"Look it up!" Vanna stormed outside where everyone gathered together to prepare to sing.

"You guys aren't of legal age yet," Tia reminded them with an eye roll.

Cole snorted at that. "If we're old enough to die protecting this world, I would think we should be old enough to drink."

"He has a point." Chance looked impressed.

"Yeah, on his head." Tia shook her head moving past the bar to the door. "Time for choir, guys."

14

Thetis

"Time for Calanda!" Gage shouted as the snow started to drift down from the sky, the sign they had been waiting for before starting to sing. The sisters were nowhere to be seen, probably back in their home waiting for the singing. This had only been their third year doing it but even so, they looked forward to it still. Even though the one person who had helped them learn it was no longer there.

They each felt the loss of Pam not being there, the one whose Greek heritage they were celebrating tonight. Of course, not only hers. After all, everyone from Sanctuary had Greek heritage, no matter how small. Even the Guardians, even though I.Q. was the one who most showed it with his dark looks. The Arions were the ones who would be singing to the mythological inhabitants of Sanctuary.

Knocking on the first door of the tree house where Elma lived, Tia and Telara shared smiles that they did their best to hide as Gage moved back and let Stella ask Elma for permission to sing for her. Elma looked over at Gage with a wistful glance before nodding to Stella, as soon as they got permission the Arions carrying their instruments started playing the familiar notes filling the air as those who had no instrument started singing…

Good evening noblemen
If this is your will,
Christ's noble birth
May I sing in your noble house?
Christ is being born today
In the town of Bethlehem.
Heavens rejoice
All of nature is happy.
Inside the cave He is being born,
In a manger for horses.
The King of all the universe
The Creator of everything.
A crowd of angels are singing,
"Ossana in excelsis",
And holly is
The faith of the shepherds.
From Persia three magi arrive
With their gifts.
A bright star shows them the way
Without any delay.
In this house we have come
May no stone ever crack.
And the landlord
May live for many years.

Elma laughed and threw candy into the crowd in thanks for the singing, another tradition of the Calanda. The candy here was not the same as you would buy in the stores back home, these treats were made by the confectioners of Thetis. Chocolate bars with nuts and berries intertwined within, and something else that is a bit tart but they were too chicken to ask what it was. Hard candies that tasted sweet, tart and bitter.

Moving from home to home they did the same thing, asking permission to sing and when it was received they would start again. They would end their song and receive treats in thanks for their song. When they got to the Grendow sisters home they couldn't wait for the treats, while they were sweet and filling, the rumor was that they made them with their own homemade ale. Although, no one seemed to feel any different after eating them, but it didn't stop the rumors.

"The songs sound so much sweeter when sung in Greek." Vanna said after singing to a family of gnomes and moving closer to the cantina, a sign they were getting close to ending the night. The others nodded, while they couldn't keep up with the Arions when they did sing in Greek, they did enjoy it and would just hum along.

"It does seem to lose some of the magic when translated into English." I.Q. said, flipping a small lightning bolt through his fingers as they neared the cantina.

"Wonder what the American carols would sound like sung in Greek," Cole mused.

"Anything sounds better as long as you aren't the one singing," Tia told him.

"Hey!" They laughed at the affronted look on his face, although that cleared up when they saw the food and drinks that lined all the tables in the cantina. It was time for the after celebrations before they left for the night to go home.

15

Sanctuary

PAM STARED around her at the only home she had ever known. A home where she was no longer welcome. She didn't realize how much she would miss it, until standing here outside the crystal caves looking around.

"I don't remember that crack in the mines." Her brother joined her. "And I thought I knew this place pretty well."

"I was doing rounds with Claw one night when Fritz drove his car into a vein of essence inside the caves. Broke right through the mountain, we could see light on the other side." Pam looked back at the cave entrance. "Fritz was already in trouble with Ira, so Claw and I managed to cover up what Fritz had done."

"No one figured it out?"

Pam lifted a shoulder dismissively. "That alcove had too many essence veins that were highly volatile so the gnomes stayed away from it."

"Really?" Flint looked back at the cave, his eyes brightening.

"No!" Pam's voice was forceful with no give.

"I'm not going to do anything." Flint flashed her one of his boyish grins, one that Stazi said always got him his way.

"Yeah, right." Pam snorted. "You would fit in with Cole and Chad."

"They must be really cool." His grin grew.

"Real annoying usually," Pam responded, moving to the gate at the end of the path.

"Sis!" Flint put his hand over heart, his face giving a faux insulted expression. "You wound me."

"Whatever." Pam moved past the stone walls turning to look at her brother who stood next to the wall but not moving towards her. Her brow furrowed. "Let's go get this over with."

"You do that," Flint told her, jumping over the stone wall, heading toward Mermaid Lake. "I have something to do."

"Flint!" Pam furiously whispered to her brother but he was already half running, half jogging away. She glared at his retreating back that shrunk in the distance. "You haven't changed one bit," she muttered and continued, "Probably going to play with Brom, who will surely go to Lucius, after they are done flirting, of course." Still grumbling about irresponsible brothers and annoying mermaids, she headed towards the Omega barracks where the Shadows are being held.

As she walked, she could hear the singing in Thetis. Her chest tightened listening to them singing the carols, calanda. Oh, how she wished she was there with them. Reaching the Omega barracks, the singing became harder to hear as the barracks was a good distance away from Thetis. She entered through a side door that was barely ever used. The spider who created a very intricate web in the top right of the door frame was an affirmation to that. No way Sassy would let that stay there; she hated spiders.

Making her way to the Shadow jail set up in the barracks, she did her best to concentrate on the mission at hand and not what she had given up. Here in the barracks she could not hear the singing from Thetis; in fact it was eerily quiet.

The jail looked the same since she was last here, with a few new additions. Every time the Guardians were at Sanctuary, Vanna would come down to the jail to see if there were any changes, see if she was able to heal those still stuck in this Shadow prison.

"How to find the one Zane wants?" she murmured to herself. Calling him Zane rather than the Shadow Master seemed less ominous, but not by much. She knew she had made a deal with the proverbial devil and she was willing to deal with those consequences. Pulling out the black, white and clear swirling crystal from her pocket she stared at it for a few moments, then lifted her hand with palm up, the crystal resting in the center. She didn't know what to expect but the crystal didn't make her wait long.

A low glow started from the center of the crystal, slowly growing brighter. The Shadows in the cages grew agitated with the glowing of the crystal. The crystal started to move in her palm, the pointed end of the tower pointing to her right. "Not the strangest thing I've done." Her voice low as she followed the crystal in her hand until she stood in front of a cell with the crystal glowing brightly, pointing straight at the Shadow in the cell and even blinking rapidly. The Shadow inside stared at her solemnly, its eyes watching her as if it understood what was going on. Not even the Shadows that had been turned from one of the Arions had that much cognitive understanding.

Looking around the area she realized this was the Shadow that Chad had said gave him the willies, Vanna always spent more time with it hoping to cure whoever was imprisoned inside. Telara had always steered clear of it, always changing the subject when asked why. "And you're the one Zane wanted," she mused.

"Zane is it? I remember when we used tae call him the Shadow Master or better yet … the enemy."

Pam jerked her head around to see Claw standing there across the room on the other side of the cells. "Claw."

"Ye remember, should I be honored?"

Pam sighed, her chest tightening. "Claw, don't be like that."

"How am I supposed tae be?"

Pam's shoulders slumped. "I don't know." She hoped to get in and out without running into anyone. She knew they wouldn't understand and she didn't know how to explain to them why she was doing what she was doing.

"What happened tae ye, Pammy?"

"Nothing!" she protested. "I'm still me, promise."

"Naw, we may not have seen eye tae eye all the time." Pam raised a sardonic brow at that remark which caused Claw to give a self-deprecating smile. "Well, hardly ever, but I always knew where ye stood."

"I stand where I always have," she told him. "With my friends."

"Darling, yer friends are all here and they miss ye."

Swallowing hard, she did her best to hold her tears from her words. "I have to do this; I wish you could understand."

"So do I, why don't ye help me understand?"

"I can't." This time she couldn't keep the emotion from her voice, causing her voice to break.

"Ye won't." He challenged her.

She didn't dispute his words as she veered the conversation to something less emotional. "You going to turn me in?"

"Naw."

"Thank you."

"I don't turn on me friends."

"Claw," Pam protested, feeling her eyes burn from tears that were attempting to sneak in.

"I call 'em as I see 'em. Ye always stood yer ground, and I always speak my mind. That used tae make us a great team." Claw turned to leave.

"Claw!" Pam protested. He paused but didn't turn. "Have you seen swirls of black in any of the crystals mined at the Sanctuary?"

This time he did turn around, his eyes hard as he looked at her. His lips tightened and he did an about face disappearing into the shadows, leaving Pam there wiping her tears.

"Okay big guy, time for us to leave here before anyone else to decides to have a reunion." Pulling out her Crim, she pressed the tip against the lock which clicked, the bars swinging open. The other Shadows fidgeted in their cells with agitation. Holding her breath, she watched the Shadow move out of its cell to stand in front of her, looking down at her. Opening her hand where the crystal still glowed, she lifted it up between them. "Behave, big boy."

"You the Shadow whisperer now?"

Closing her eyes, Pam silently berated herself for getting snuck up on, not only once, but twice. Keeping the crystal tower in view of the Shadow, she turned to see Telara staring at her from the open doorway. Claw had looked forlorn at finding her here but Telara looked angry at seeing her. "Not really, just taking him home."

"You know I can't allow that." Her Rotary started to slowly glow. "Neither of you are leaving. The Shadow will go back to its cell and you're going to explain what the hell is going on with you."

"Afraid I can't." Pam hated herself as she saw the strain on Telara's face. Telara always wore her emotions on her sleeve and Pam knew this had to be hurting her friend, who had been through more than anyone should at her age. "I wish I could, just know I'm still on your side."

"Seriously? You're working for the man trying to kill us!"

"It's not that simple!"

"Then make it that simple!" The pain in Telara's voice resonated with Pam who was doing her best not to lose it before she got out of her. "Tell me what is going on! Tell me that you haven't turned on us!"

"I can't."

"You won't!"

Shaking her head, Pam moved to walk away from the cells with the lone free Shadow following her obediently. She hadn't gotten very far before Telara appeared from above her, landing right in front of her. Pam looked back to where Telara had stood only moments before on the other side of the room. "Flying? Someone's getting the hang of their powers."

"You would know all about it if you hadn't left. You would also know they are taking away our family's memories of us after we graduate." When Pam said nothing, she continued, "You would know Hades kidnapped Lucius and the Leaders won't let us save him." Her voice broke before she could stop it.

"I'm sorry, I really am."

"We don't need your pity, we need you to come home."

"I can't."

"I'm not letting you leave." Her Rotary started to glow brighter, causing the Shadows in the cells to grow anxious.

"Not your choice, sweets." They both turned around just as Flint placed a dark, circular, flat crystal on the nearest cell to him. As soon as the crystal touched the metal bars all the cells opened around them and chaos erupted.

"Flint!" Pam frowned at him but he grabbed her arm, pulling her away as Telara created force shields to stop the Shadows who were attempting to swarm her. Shouts could be heard as the other Guardians and Arions filled into the Omega's barracks. "You're putting them in danger."

"They'll be fine, just distracted." He practically dragged her behind him as he headed for the caves.

"You don't know that." Pam attempted to look back but her brother kept pulling her past the stone walls around the caves, to the crack in the cave walls and their way out of Sanctuary. Once they got past the Sanctuary boundaries, the shadows encased them so that they could see no light. When the shadows dissipated Pam saw the dying landscape of the Shadow's lair. Turning to her brother, Pam forgot what she was going to say when she saw something glinting in his hand. "What is that?" She reached for it but Flint moved his hand out of her reach, moving forward towards the porch, turning around grinning at her as he walked backwards.

"Just a little memento from the Guardians' secret room." He

tossed the silver ball in the air, catching it again before turning around still moving forward.

Pam frowned at his words that took a few moments for them to sink in, but when they did her stomach took a nose dive straight down before she felt the slow burning anger begin to simmer. "Is that Streak?" She asked him slowly, her eyes narrowing on him. "Is that Vanna's squirrel?"

Flint looked down at the silver ball in his hand. "Don't look like no squirrel to me."

"Take it back!" she told him, moving forward towards him with dark looks.

"Too late," he told her, still moving backwards.

"Why?" She kept moving forward, her eyes on the silver ball as she moved, waiting for any opening to grab it.

"Zane ordered this acquisition to be done, even above your Shadow friend." He nodded towards the Shadow that followed her silently.

Her lips pressed together as her eyes narrowed on him. "Why does he want Streak?"

Flint shrugged. "Ask him." Turning back to walk forward to the house. "Let's go and give Zane our loot so we can get some grub."

"Wait!" Pam stopped him by grabbing his arm. He frowned at her. "Did you know Hades took Lucius?" He looked away quickly, but not before Pam saw that guilt on his face. "You did!" she accused.

Flint sighed. "It doesn't matter Pam."

"What do you mean, it doesn't matter?" Her hands went to her hips. "The leaders won't even let Telara and the others try to rescue him."

"Zane didn't think it was necessary to tell you that." Flint told her.

"Really? Sounds like being back at Sanctuary, you thought Zane was going to be more transparent. Or were those words? Do as I say, not as I do?"

"Let Sanctuary deal with their problems." He turned, striding away with his long legs. "You can ask Zane his reasons for keeping it secret later."

"I will," Pam said grimly as she followed him with the Shadow in tow, her gaze still dark as she glared at his back. She knew that when Vanna discovered Streak gone, she would be hurt. If she had known what Flint was up to when he ran off, she would've stopped him. Vanna will never forgive for that treachery, for being the sweetest one of the bunch, she could hold a grudge longer than most. Good thing she wasn't one of the Hatfields or McCoys or else that feud would've never ended.

16

Sanctuary

"They're getting away!" A burst of cold air followed Chad's warning as ice shards erupted in front of three of the Shadows that were attempting to disappear through the shadows. They had already lost two but were doing the best to retain the rest.

"Some light would help!" Cole looked at Telara as he managed to contain two out of three Shadows in a ring of fire as the third slipped away through the Shadows.

She frowned at him, barely missing the giant Shadow that lumbered at her. "What do you want me to do? I'm not a light-bulb. Fires make light too, you know."

"They also burn down buildings," Cole countered dryly. "You on the other hand can make others see what isn't there and won't burn down the building in the process."

Telara stared at him as comprehension dawned and she felt chagrined.

"Now would be a good time!" Tia not so subtly nudged her while creating two miniature tornados that sucked up a Shadow each before tossing them back into a cell.

Telara took a deep breath, doing her best to not think about how it was Zane who taught her how to do this, then imagined the room flooded with light. Screams filled the room as the Shadows attempted to hide from the light. "You got your light, now get those Shadows back in containment," she shouted as she used her power to mentally push one of the Shadows into the nearest cell, slamming the door on it.

Turning around, she quickly sidestepped before a Shadow was chased into a cell by a rose bush shooting thorns. After lighting up the room, they managed to get the remaining Shadows back in their cells with only losing a total of four Shadows. Looking around Telara let out a sigh before plopping down in a nearby chair. She looked up at the others in the room, Gage stared around with a bewildered expression. No one knew exactly how to feel or act after Pam left.

"Why didn't the alarms go off?" Chance bent over, his hands clenching his knees.

"Because they aren't Shadows, our alarms are configured for Shadows, not Arions." Gage leaned back against the nearest wall, breathing hard. "Looks like we need to do some adjusting."

17

Shadow's Lair

THE BLACKNESS SWIRLED within the crystal tower that now sat on Zane's desk in his room deep within the bowels of the house, hidden from everyone but Zane and Lyra. Although there were times Zane wouldn't mind being the only one who had access, Lyra wasn't always welcome there. If Zane were being honest with himself, he never wanted her there but unfortunately, they had codependency issues. Zane looked over at the Shadow who stood in the corner watching him with narrowed eyes that would pierce him through the heart if they could.

"Hello again, dear friend," Zane looked at the Shadow, no smile on his face. "I wonder if you can understand what is going on around you? Never having gone through the Shadow transformation myself, I wouldn't know." The Shadow never once moved but its expression seemed to grow darker, if that was possible on a creature of pure darkness. It could be Zane imagined the emotions he would expect from the person beneath the darkness. "Not sure if it is my imagination or if you are truly glowering at me, but if so then I would guess you can understand me just fine, Plax."

The Shadow jerked at the name, as if it understood. "Well, if you can understand me then I need you to know I'm sorry for all that has happened but I couldn't let what the Gods did destroy my family." No reaction from the Shadow in the corner, either the earlier reactions were truly a figment of Zane's imagination or it was doing it on purpose. "I don't expect you to understand, you don't know what truly happened. None of you do, none of you would understand." Zane held out his hand and the black crystal tower slowly hovered from its place on his desk to land squarely in the palm of his hand. "My daughter was murdered because she was the key to reuniting the crystals; she didn't even know anything of the prophecy, but the gods did and they feared anyone having more power than them."

Standing up and moving to the fireplace in his room he stared down into the flickering flames. "If they discovered the truth, they wouldn't have let any of our descendants live at all. Something that I guess I do owe to Lucius, though there is much that he has yet to answer for." Looking down at the constant moving silver sphere in the glass box that Flint had pilfered for him. "We all have a lot to answer for, and that day is coming closer."

18

Shadow's Lair

PAM SAT OUTSIDE amongst the dead trees and plants that littered the landscape around the house. Walking around barefoot wasn't advisable, the dead grass and plants were so brittle that they could pierce the skin. There were old iron benches outside with black peeling paint, while the air was depressed, Pam found being out here to be more comfortable than inside the house. She sat on one of those benches, her legs pulled up to her chest with her arms wrapped around them.

"It's a lot warmer in the house."

Pam didn't even turn around to acknowledge her brother, she was still chafed at him over what happened at Sanctuary. "It's also crowded." She knew joining her brother and Zane meant she would have to put up with being around the Shadows but she didn't think she would ever get as comfortable as her brother has with being in such close proximity on a day-to-day basis.

"Sis, you knew that was part of the deal."

"Well, maybe I don't like that part of the deal." She stared straight ahead, not turning to acknowledge her brother who stood next to her, leaning against a tree. His posture had definitely declined since defected to the Shadow side.

"Pam —"

Pam held up a hand to silence him. "I know, I know. I just need some space. Okay?"

She heard him sigh. "Okay. I just came out to give you this." She turned and saw a box wrapped in wrapping.

"Christmas isn't until tomorrow," she told him.

"It's not from me."

"Huh?"

"Claw asked me to give this to you." He nodded at her wide eyes. "I ran into him on my way to get you out of there. The man looked pretty broken up," he told her as he handed her the box, turning away to give her some privacy.

Her fingers pulled at the ribbons slowly watching them fall away from the box in a glittering wave. Opening up the box she saw a silver necklace with one charm, a piece of bread with a gold coin in the center. A note on the top of the box read: I know the Vasilopita isn't until New Year's Eve but since we won't be together, I wanted you to have this and know I will be thinking of you. Even though the note was written in perfect English, she still heard it in Claw's heavy accent. She didn't stop the single tear that escaped and rolled down her cheek.

19

Hades' Realm

THUD!

Lucius could barely feel the pain from his fist hitting the stone wall of the prison Hades kept him. A cave deep in the realm of Tartarus, so deep that would be no chance of any of the other gods discovering him. Something he was positive was done on purpose.

"Would you like me to turn the channel" Hades' mocking voice had him gritting his teeth. Since Lucius was unable to leave this prison, Hades left him a way to see what was happening in the outside world. Taking malicious delight in the pain Lucius felt at seeing the turmoil happening back in Sanctuary.

He turned to stare at the god who watched him carefully. "Tartarus, Hades? You wouldn't be trying to hide the fact that you are holding me here, now would you?"

Hades snorted. "This is my realm; I will keep you where I choose. I told you that you were playing a dangerous game. Should've listened to me."

"The question is, whom is it dangerous for? Me? Or you?"

Hades moved to stand in front of the vision in the wall where

Lucius had watched Pam and her brother only moments before. "Looks like your precious mortals are falling apart without you there to play puppet master." He sneered at him. "Or should I say chess master."

"They will be just fine without me, you'll see. Not only that but they will also defeat her and Zane as well." Lucius told him. "Don't think that I didn't notice your little tactic to change the topic. You know, what I don't understand is why you would put yourself at risk with the other gods over a fling." Lucius watched Hades closely as he looked into the portal, where the vision changed from the somber Pam to Lyra, sitting in her room dressed in that cloak, crooning to a crystal flower.

"You know nothing." Hades growled, sounding barely human.

"I know that because you got distracted by a pretty face, I lost my son, his wife and my granddaughter." Lucius fired back, his voice strained with emotion.

Hades' lip curled up. "You got your precious granddaughter back though, didn't you? Even though you swore that the prophecy had been broken."

"If the gods knew the prophecy was still intact, they would've killed off the Guardians before they had a chance to breathe their first breath, and then the Shadow Master would've destroyed your world."

"You mean, your son." Hades threw back at him.

Lucius took a shaky breath. "Yes, my son. My son who was created by all the damage Lyra did."

"You know nothing about her." Hades turned on Lucius, his eyes becoming flames of blue.

"I know she killed her first husband." Lucius stared at him, his gaze as hard as his voice.

Hades snorted. "The man probably deserved it."

"No, he was a good man," Lucius told him, swallowing hard. "He wanted to help his kingdom, not dominate it. His values didn't align with hers, so after she got what she wanted from him, she killed him."

"And what was it she wanted?" Hades practically sneered.

"A crown. He was a king who fell for her lies and deceit."

"And you know this how? Don't tell me those pathetic Paladins told you these stories to make their atrocities seem valid?" Hades looked down on him with a haughty look.

"No, I know this because he was my father," Lucius told him simply while Hades stared at him as if in shock. "Yeah, Lyra is my mother. Not that either of us like to admit it. She sees too much of my father in me, and every time I look at her, I see my father's lifeless eyes."

Hades stared at him as the flames in his eyes disappeared with a little pop. Lucius wasn't sure if he should back away or just stand there and let the god do what he will. It wasn't like Lucius could stop him anyways. Before Lucius could say another word, Hades was gone, barely a cloud of smoke left behind. Lucius looked around him and sighed. "Isn't that like a god, they can't win an argument so they leave."

20

Bungalow

"Hurry up Telly!" Cole shouted as she ran up the stairs to her room in their Bungalow to grab her coat, hat and gloves before they head back to the winter wonderland at home.

"Be right there," she shouted back as she grabbed her coat off her bed. A thudding sound had her turning around to look at the floor by her bed where a colorfully wrapped box lay on its side. Looking around her room she saw no one there, looking back down at the box she frowned. Taking in a deep breath she bent down to pick it up. "Where did you come from?" she murmured before gasping and almost dropping the box on the floor for the second time.

There in front of her was Flint, or at least an illusion of Flint. Not a solid illusion either, it was like watching a 3D projection walking right in front of her into her room. She watched as he placed the box on her bed, then turned as if he looked right at her with that infuriating smile of his, as if he knew she stood there. Then he was gone. Looking back down at the box she wasn't sure if she should open it.

"Hey Telly, we're going to be late getting home." Tia appeared in the doorway with everyone else holding up their arms if looking at imaginary watches.

"What's that?" I.Q. gestured to the present in her hand.

"A present that Flint left in my room," she finished feebly.

"How do you know it was Flint?" Tia looked around the present to see if there was a card on it.

"I saw him." She sighed when they still looked confused. "I'll explain later. Right now, I'm not sure if I should even open the gift."

"Why not?" Telara looked up at I.Q., who lifted a shoulder in a shrug. "It's for you, isn't it?" She nodded. "We're right here with you, unless you would rather us leave."

"No." She shook her head. "I'd rather you stayed." Taking a deep breath she unwrapped the box, frowning at the purple crystal bowl she lifted from the box with the jagged sides.

"That looks familiar," Vanna murmured as she moved closer.

"Yeah, Zane had one on his desk," Telara said, putting the bowl back in the box and placing it on the stand next to her bed. "C'mon, we have to get going."

"What about…" Chance gestured to the present.

"It can stay there." Telara said dismissively as she hurried out of her room. "Let's go home."

21

Shadow's Lair

"Ungh!" one of the lumbering shapeshifting Shadows grunted as it moved to let the little Shadow, who was singing and hopping around past him. Kele hummed as she hopped from foot to foot, her dark pigtails swaying with her movements, moving down the hallway as other Shadows moved out of her way. Bac and Knucker looked out of the rooms they had been, down the hallway to see their sister Shadow singing and dancing once again.

They moved to follow her closely, not paying one bit attention to the larger Shadows, watching Kele as she danced and stomped down the hallway.

"Naughty Shadows ... Evil Shadows ... great big blobs of doom!"

"Controlled Shadows ... Scary Shadows ... Gloom! Gloom! Gloom!"

ABOUT THE AUTHOR

TL Shively is an award-winning author who loves her husband and three boys; they are not only a lot of her inspiration but also her greatest supporters. She is very outnumbered in a house full of boys; even their dog is male.

Her whole life has been full of stories that used to be only in her head, entertaining her when she was younger and lived in the country where the nearest neighbor was miles down the road. It wasn't until she was much older that she finally put these stories down on paper, and it was the Sanctuary Guardian's story that came out.

She loves anything fantasy: gaming, reading, writing, knick-knacks, you name it. She loves crafting of almost any kind and comes from a very artistic family.

THANK YOU

A special thank you to my Kele and the creator of the Shadow's song.